If I Were Your Father

Margaret Park Bridges

Illustrated by Kady MacDonald Denton

Morrow Junior Books

NEW YORK

For Alan,
and for his father, Ed, who was like a father to me.
—M. P. B.

For W.T.D.
—K.M.D.

Watercolors were used for the full-color illustrations.
The text type is 15-point Opti Adrift.

Text copyright © 1999 by Margaret Park Bridges
Illustrations copyright © 1999 by Kady MacDonald Denton

Published by Morrow Junior Books
a division of William Morrow and Company, Inc.
1350 Avenue of the Americas, New York, NY 10019
www.williammorrow.com

Printed in Singapore at Tien Wah Press.

10 9 8 7 6 5 4 3 2 1

Library of Congress Cataloging-in-Publication Data
Bridges, Margaret Park.
If I were your father / Margaret Park Bridges; illustrated by Kady MacDonald Denton.
p. cm.
Summary: A boy tells his father all the special things he would
do for him if their positions were reversed and he was the father.
ISBN 0-688-15192-2 (trade)—ISBN 0-688-15193-0 (library)
[1. Father and child—Fiction.]   I. Denton, Kady MacDonald, ill.   II. Title.
PZ7.B7619If 1999   [E]—dc21   98-24131   CIP   AC

Daddy, do you like being my father?

Of course, buddy. I love you.

How did you learn to be a father, Daddy? Did you go to school?

Yes, but no one taught me THAT.

I could teach you, Daddy.

Teach me how to be a good father?

Yes. We could trade places.

Okay, buddy. What would you do if you were my father?

If I were your father, I'd let you shave me
with whipped cream in the morning.

And wash your hair with maple syrup?

And brush my teeth with cake frosting!

If I were your father, I would take you fishing on a school day.

Could we keep the fish in our little swimming pool?

No. We'd throw them back so their families wouldn't worry.

If I were your father, I'd get you a dog bigger than you.

That I could ride like a horse?

Yes, all the way to the grocery store and back.

If I were your father, I would cut your sandwiches into funny shapes.

Like cars and butterflies and dinosaurs?

They taste better that way.

If I were your father, I would bring you to my office and let you push all the buttons on the elevator.

And run down the hallways?

Run and do cartwheels!

If I were your father, I'd take you hunting for buried treasure.

Would we find it?

Of course—we'd hide so much in our pockets that our pants would fall down!

If I were your father,
I wouldn't yell if you stood in front of the TV while I was watching a game.

Even if you
missed a home run
in the World Series?

Even if I missed a whole game.

If I were your father, I'd take you to the zoo,
the playground, the library,
and the movies all in one day.

What if I was so tired
that I fell asleep before dinner?

I'd save your dinner for breakfast.

If I were your father,
I'd give you a bath with so many bubbles I couldn't see you.

What if I got lost?

I'd send out the navy to find you!

If I were your father, I would buy us matching pajamas.

So no one could
tell us apart?

So we could be best buddies and do everything the same together.

If I were your father,
I'd tuck you in bed so tight the covers would never come loose.

But what if I had to go to the bathroom?

You'd slide out like a letter from an envelope.

If I were your father, I'd play you the guitar at bedtime every night.

And sing songs?

Like cowboys around a campfire.

If I were your father,
I'd tell you stories about my adventures when I was little.

About how you got into trouble?

About how I got OUT of it!
And if I were your father, I'd let you make all your own decisions.

What if I
made mistakes?

I'd think you were brave to try. And I'd help you whenever you needed me.

Well, you certainly have some great ideas, buddy.
You'll be a good father someday.

But, Daddy?

Yes?

How can I remember all that when I'm big?

Don't worry, buddy. I'll be there to remind you.

If I were your father, I'd take you hunting for buried treasure.

Would we find it?

Of course—we'd hide so much in our pockets that our pants would fall down!

If I were your father,
I wouldn't yell if you stood in front of the TV while I was watching a game.

Even if you
missed a home run
in the World Series?

Even if I missed a whole game.

If I were your father, I'd take you to the zoo,
the playground, the library,
and the movies all in one day.

What if I was so tired
that I fell asleep before dinner?

I'd save your dinner for breakfast.

If I were your father,
I'd give you a bath with so many bubbles I couldn't see you.

What if I got lost?

I'd send out the navy to find you!

If I were your father, I would buy us matching pajamas.

So no one could
tell us apart?

So we could be best buddies and do everything the same together.

If I were your father,
I'd tuck you in bed so tight the covers would never come loose.

But what if I had to go to the bathroom?

You'd slide out like a letter from an envelope.

If I were your father, I'd play you the guitar at bedtime every night.

And sing songs?

Like cowboys around a campfire.

If I were your father,
I'd tell you stories about my adventures when I was little.

About how you got into trouble?

About how I got OUT of it!
And if I were your father, I'd let you make all your own decisions.

What if I made mistakes?

I'd think you were brave to try. And I'd help you whenever you needed me.

Well, you certainly have some great ideas, buddy.
You'll be a good father someday.

But, Daddy?

Yes?

How can I remember all that when I'm big?

Don't worry, buddy. I'll be there to remind you.